FRIGHTFUL FAMILIES

CHEF SHOCKER

SUE MONGREDIEN • TERESA MURFIN

ORCHARD BOOKS

Amy Hitchin loved her food. So did her mum. So did her dad. Mr and Mrs Hitchin were chefs. They ran a restaurant in town, called Hitchins' Kitchen. It was a very peculiar restaurant.

You couldn't get fish and chips there.

You couldn't order a steak there.

They didn't even serve chocolate pudding and ice cream.

Instead, Mr and Mrs Hitchin cooked...
different food. Food that most people had
never even dreamed of eating, like Brussel
sprouts in custard. Or cauliflower cake, with
mint jam. Or beetroot and banana soup.

Trendy critics marvelled at the menu.

"So experimental!"

"So outrageous!"

"So twenty-first century!"

Other people weren't quite so impressed.

And whenever any children were taken
to the restaurant, it was quite clear what
they thought.

Amy, of course, was different. She had grown up eating strange food. As a baby, her parents had mashed up banana with garlic parsnips – and she'd wolfed it down.

As a toddler, she'd scoffed killer-hot curries for breakfast.

By the time she went to school, she could cook all sorts of things. Her mushroom meringues melted in the mouth and her sultana omelettes were egg-cellent!

But ever since she had started school, Amy had begun to notice that her parents weren't like all the other parents. In fact, she was starting to realise that they were a teeny weeny bit...unusual.

Amy first noticed this when they began a new class project about food. Everyone had to take it in turns to stand up and tell the class what food they liked best.

"My favourite food is pizza," said Nathan, licking his lips.

"Mine is ice cream," said Molly dreamily.

"My favourite food is cabbage toffee," said Amy. She could just imagine the perfect green cubes...mmmm...

The whole class burst out laughing. "Cabbage *toffee*?" some of the boys hooted. "Ugh!"

"Don't be silly, dear," Amy's teacher said. "What is your favourite food really?"

Amy's face turned tomato red. She felt confused. Why was everybody laughing? "Um...pizza," she fibbed.

That was the first time Amy thought that her parents' cooking might be rather different. The second time was when she invited a friend, Emily, home for tea.

"Brains on toast all right, girls?" Mrs Hitchin had smiled, as Amy and Emily took their shoes and coats off.

Emily turned as white as flour. "Don't you
mean *beans* on toast?" she had gulped.

"No, brains, dear," Mrs Hitchin told her.
"Sheep's brains. With just a little bit of
marmalade and..."

Emily was looking as green as a Brussel sprout. "I've just remembered – I've got a dentist's appointment," she gabbled, putting her shoes back on quickly. "Gotta go. Bye, Amy!"

"Was it something I said, Pumpkin?"
Amy's mum wondered, frowning.

"I'm not sure," Amy replied. She watched
the door bang behind Emily. "Maybe she's
a vegetarian."

The next day, Amy heard the whispers going around the class. "*Brains* on *toast*! Emily said she was nearly sick!"

Amy felt so embarrassed, her cheeks turned as red as a chilli pepper.

Next time she asked somebody home for tea, she vowed *she* would do the cooking.

Then, one morning, things got a whole lot worse. A letter arrived for Mr and Mrs Hitchin, which said:

We're delighted to confirm the filming dates for the Life Swap *programme, in which you will be swapping places with the kitchen staff of Donchester Primary School for a week...*

Amy gasped. Donchester Primary School? That was *her* school! Did that mean...?

"Isn't it wonderful?" her mum giggled. "Your dad and I are going to be cooking your school dinners for a whole week!"

Amy was so shocked she could hardly eat her boiled ostrich egg. She glanced at the filming dates in the letter. Oh, no. Next week! Filming started next week!

"We'll plan the menu tonight," her dad said gleefully. "What do you think, Amy? Reckon the kids will like our mushy pea jelly?"

As everyone sat down for lunch on Monday, Amy had butterflies. The camera crew were there. The dinner tables were all full. And there was a very strange smell coming from the school kitchen. She really hoped it wasn't...

"Snail stew!" smiled her mum, coming out of the kitchen. She put one dish on every table. There was a *SCRAPE!* as every single child pushed their chair back in horror.

There was a GASP! as every single child smelled the savoury snaily smell. Then there was a dead silence. You could have heard a breadcrumb drop.

"I don't want to eat snails," a girl wailed.

"And here are the veggies," Amy's dad said. He had a tray piled high with bowls. "Butterscotch broccoli, carrot mousse and ice-cold nice-cold spinach sorbet."

"I'll just get the pilchard pickle," Mrs Hitchin said. "Then you can all start."

"Is this a joke?" Leo Webster, the toughest boy in school asked. A cameraman wheeled around to film him speaking. "We always have bangers and mash on a Monday."

"And onion gravy," someone else chipped in. "Where's the onion gravy?"

Mr and Mrs Hitchin laughed. "Oh dear," said Mr Hitchin.

"Didn't anybody tell you?" Mrs Hitchin asked. "We don't cook things like *bangers and mash*. We're international chefs! And for this week only, we're cooking for you." She wiped her hands on her apron proudly. "You know, you're very lucky."

All eyes swivelled across to the dishes of snail stew, still untouched.

Lucky? The Donchester Primary children didn't feel lucky. In fact, they wished their old dinner ladies would come straight back!

The school dinner ladies, meanwhile, had taken over Hitchins' Kitchen. They were cooking their usual Monday meal – bangers and mash, with oodles of onion gravy. And for pudding? Why, it was jam sponge, of course. With gallons of vanilla custard.

Delicious smells drifted out from the restaurant. The news spread like wildfire. A new menu at Hitchins' Kitchen – for one week only! Nobody could resist the smell of sizzling sausages or steaming jam sponge. The waiters were rushed off their feet!

It was the same on Tuesday. The school
dinner ladies cooked fish fingers and peas at
the restaurant, which went down a storm.

The schoolchildren, meanwhile, had
mincemeat marshmallows with gherkin
gravy, followed by cabbage candy floss.

There were a lot of hungry tummies in
school that afternoon.

Amy really wished her parents had picked another school to do their life swap. Everybody seemed to be blaming *her* for it!

"I've told the TV company that if we have to *look* at another snail, the whole school is going to bring in packed lunches," Leo Webster said to her loudly.

"Same goes for the cabbage candy floss,"
his mate Jasper complained. "Can't you get
them to cook us something normal, Amy?"

Amy shrugged her shoulders. "But their
food is *nice*, honestly. If you just tasted it,
you might like it..."

"Taste it? What, eat snails?" Leo asked. He pulled a face. "Not likely. It's Wednesday tomorrow. That's steak and kidney pudding day. Can't you ask them to make it for us?"

"OK," Amy promised. "I'll try. But I don't know if it'll make any difference."

That evening, over a yummy tea of kipper truffles, Amy asked, "Have you thought about what you're cooking tomorrow? Only—"

"Octopus," Mrs Hitchin replied cheerfully. "Lightly fried with garlic, grapefruit juice and sugar puffs."

Amy winced. She could just imagine Leo's
face when the plate was put down in front of
him! "We usually have steak and kidney
pudding, you see," she said. "It's everybody's
favourite. And—"

"They'll have a new favourite tomorrow,
then, won't they?" beamed Mr Hitchin. "We
haven't even told you the pudding yet – it's
mackerel meringue!"

"Right," said Amy, trying not to sigh. The Hitchins' mackerel meringue was pretty tasty. *She* knew that. But would anybody else at school agree?

No, was the answer to that question, though a few people scraped off the mackerel mousse and nibbled at the meringue underneath.

There was a whole trough full of leftovers for the Donchester Farm pigs that day. They thought they were in piggy heaven!

After turnip pancakes and haggis cookies
on Thursday, Amy was starting to despair.
Leo and Jasper decided to organise a protest
against the Hitchins' school lunches. They'd
asked the TV people to help them make
banners, posters and stickers for everyone.

"Sorry, Amy," Jasper said. "I know they're your mum and dad. But we can't face any more freaky food."

Amy thought hard all afternoon. She thought all the way through her music lesson. She thought all the way through break-time, and all the way through PE. And then she came up with an idea.

"Mum, Dad, can we eat out tonight?" she
said when she got home from school.

Mr Hitchin was about to start cutting up
a large pumpkin. "Eat out?" he echoed. He
prodded the pumpkin. "That's not a bad
idea, Cookie. This pumpkin isn't quite ripe."

"We could try that new African restaurant in town," Mrs Hitchin said. "I've heard they do a lovely curried goat."

"Or maybe Hungry Hungary?" Mr Hitchin suggested. "I quite fancy a bowl of goulash."

Amy took a deep breath and crossed her fingers behind her back. "How about going to *your* restaurant and seeing what the dinner ladies are cooking tonight?"

Mr Hitchin laughed. "I don't think so," he said. "What – chicken nuggets and chips? I think we can do better than that."

Amy crossed more of her fingers. "School dinners aren't just chicken nuggets, Dad," she said. "We have lots of nice things. Sausages and pies and sponge puddings..."

Mrs Hitchin was nodding thoughtfully.
"We should probably give it a try, dear," she
said to Mr Hitchin. "After all, it *is* our
restaurant. I know it's not exactly our style
of cooking, but..."

"PLEASE!" Amy put in quickly, crossing her arms, legs, fingers and toes.

Mr Hitchin smiled. "All right," he said. "Let's go and see what they've done to our restaurant. I hope they haven't *totally* ruined our reputation!"

When the Hitchins arrived at the restaurant, they were shocked to see an enormous queue of people waiting outside. The TV camera crew were interviewing them. "It's roast chicken tonight," the Hitchins heard somebody saying happily.

"Treacle pudding for afters, too,"
somebody else said, sighing with pleasure.
"With hot ginger custard. Mm-mmm!"

"I've been here every night this week,"
a third person said into the camera.
"The food is fantastic!"

The Hitchins waited half an hour for a table. They had never seen the restaurant so full! Once inside, they sat down to a full roast dinner.

"Very ordinary looking," Mr Hitchin commented in disappointment. Then he took a mouthful of roast potato...

...And a look of surprise spread across his face. It was...well, actually, it was delicious! Truly delicious!

"This chicken is a work of art," Mrs Hitchin marvelled, munching away. "Yet it's so...plain! Who would have thought it?"

The Hitchins cleared their plates within seconds. Then it was time for the treacle pudding and custard.

The Hitchins fell silent as they gobbled up every last gorgeous, gooey mouthful. Mrs Hitchin had seconds. And Mr Hitchin had thirds! "This is the finest dessert I have ever had in my life!" he declared, licking his spoon clean in wonder. "Excellent!"

Amy couldn't stop smiling. In fact, she was
finding it hard not to giggle. Maybe her
parents had seen the light and they would start
cooking normal things! Maybe she'd even get
a proper birthday cake this year with *chocolate*
decorations, rather than sugared slugs!

"Hey, you know, I bet you two could cook treacle pudding like this," she said. She tried to sound as if the idea had only just come to her. "After all, you *are* international chefs." She smiled brightly. "You could even cook this tomorrow, for the last school lunch!"

"We could, couldn't we?" Mrs Hitchin said thoughtfully.

Mr Hitchin called the waitress over. "Another bowl of the treacle pudding, please," he said. "And the recipe, too!"

Amy beamed. Her plan was working!

The next day was Friday. As soon as Amy walked into the classroom, she felt everyone turn to look at her. "Well?" the class asked.

Amy grinned. "Don't worry," she told them. "I think we're in for a normal lunch today at last!"

Everyone cheered, and Amy sat down at her desk feeling happier than she had done all week. Happy – and relieved. It was hard work, having embarrassing parents!

At lunchtime, there was a round of applause when Mrs Hitchin brought out plates of chicken and chips. OK, so nobody touched the cauliflower ketchup, but you couldn't have everything.

A silence had fallen over the dining room, but for the first time all week, it was because the children were all busily eating.

Amy finished her last chip and looked around. Everybody was smiling. What would be for pudding? The children couldn't help guessing excitedly. Strawberry tart? Jam roly-poly? Chocolate mousse?

Mr Hitchin came out of the kitchen, with the tray of puddings. "And now a special treat for everybody," he said. "It's the first time I've tried this recipe so I hope you like it."

Amy grinned. Good old Dad. She knew he could do it!

"It's...treacle pudding," he said.

"With gravy ice cream," Mrs Hitchen added proudly, handing around bowls. Amy stared at the brown ice cream on the lovely treacle sponge. Even to her, it looked vile!

Across the table, she caught Leo's eye. He winked. "Face it, Amy – your mum and dad are never going to be *that* normal," he said.

Amy laughed. "I know," she said. "Cheesy sprinkles, anyone?"

FRIGHTFUL FAMILIES

WRITTEN BY SUE MONGREDIEN • ILLUSTRATED BY TERESA MURFIN

Explorer Trauma	1 84362 571 7
Headmaster Disaster	1 84362 572 5
Millionaire Mayhem	1 84362 573 3
Clown Calamity	1 84362 574 1
Popstar Panic	1 84362 575 X
Football-mad Dad	1 84362 576 8
Chef Shocker	1 84362 577 6
Astronerds	1 84362 803 1

All priced at £3.99

Frightful Families are available from all good book shops, or can be ordered direct from the publisher: Orchard Books, PO BOX 29, Douglas IM99 1BQ
Credit card orders please telephone 01624 836000
or fax 01624 837033 or visit our Internet site: www.wattspub.co.uk
or e-mail: bookshop@enterprise.net for details.

To order please quote title, author and ISBN
and your full name and address.
Cheques and postal orders should be made payable to 'Bookpost plc.'
Postage and packing is FREE within the UK
(overseas customers should add £1.00 per book).
Prices and availability are subject to change.